KIDS CAN'T STOP READING THE *CHOOSE YOUR OWN ADVENTURE*® STORIES!

"I like *Choose Your Own Adventure*® books because they're full of surprises. I can't wait to read more."
—Cary Romanos, age 12

"Makes you think thoroughly before making a decision."
—Hassan Stevenson, age 11

"I have read five different stories in one night and that's a record for me. The different endings are fun."
—Timmy Sullivan, age 9

"It's great fun! I like the idea of making my own decisions."
—Anthony Ziccardi, age 11

AND TEACHERS LIKE THIS SERIES, TOO!

"We have read and reread, wore thin, loved, loaned, bought for others, and donated to school libraries, the *Choose Your Own Adventure*® books."

CHOOSE YOUR OWN ADVENTURE®— AND MAKE READING MORE FUN!

D0090143

Bantam Books in the Choose Your Own Adventure® Series
Ask your bookseller for the books you have missed

Choose Your Own Adventure® Books for younger readers

BY BALLOON TO THE SAHARA

D. TERMAN

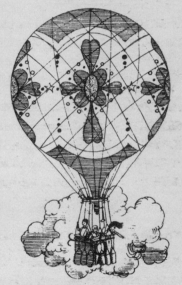

ILLUSTRATED BY PAUL GRANGER

BANTAM BOOKS
TORONTO · NEW YORK · LONDON · SYDNEY

RL 4, Age 10 and up

BY BALLOON TO THE SAHARA
A Bantam Book / July 1979

2nd printing . . . December 1979	6th printing . . . . . February 1981
3rd printing . . . . May 1980	7th printing . . . . July 1981
4th printing . . . . . . August 1980	8th printing . . . . . January 1982
5th printing . . . . . October 1980	9th printing . . . . . January 1982
	10th printing . . . . . August 1982		

CHOOSE YOUR OWN ADVENTURE® is a
trademark of Bantam Books, Inc.

Original conception of Edward Packard

Illustrations by Paul Granger

ISBN 0-553-23183-9

Published simultaneously in the United States and Canada

Bantam Books are published by Bantam Books, Inc. Its trade-
mark, consisting of the words "Bantam Books" and the por-
trayal of a rooster, is Registered in U.S. Patent and Trademark
Office and in other countries. Marca Registrada. Bantam
Books, Inc., 666 Fifth Avenue, New York, New York 10103.

PRINTED IN THE UNITED STATES OF AMERICA

O   19   18   17   16   15   14   13   12   11

With love
to my daughter
Christine M. Terman

WARNING!!!!

Do not read this book straight through from beginning to end! These pages contain many different adventures you can have on your trip in a balloon. From time to time as you read along, you will be asked to make a choice. Your choice may lead to success or disaster!

The adventures you take are a result of your choice. *You* are responsible because *you* choose! After you make your choice follow the instructions to see what happens to you next.

Remember—you cannot go back! Think carefully before you make a move! One mistake can be your last . . . or it *may* lead you to fame and fortune!

You are visiting France with your two best friends, Peter and Sarah. For a lark, you all rent a balloon. Peter packs a picnic basket and Sarah buys a large jug of fresh milk. Harry, your dog, begs to come along and you let him scramble in. At last, you lift off and start your adventure. To the north, you can see the white-capped Alps and to the south, the blue waters of the Mediterranean Sea. As you drift over villages, people look up and wave at you. Suddenly, you notice storm clouds approaching from the north.

If you act now, you can release gas from the balloon and land before the storm overtakes you. If this is your choice, turn to page 2.

Perhaps the storm will pass quickly. Maybe you can ride it out. If this is what you decide to do, turn to page 3.

You pull on the cord releasing some of the gas, allowing you to descend. Nothing happens! The storm clouds are coming closer, and the gentle wind has now turned into a howling gale. The coast is near. You must release some of the gas and settle to earth or you will be swept out to sea. Sarah says, "Let's pull harder. The valve is stuck."

But Peter pulls out his jackknife. The situation is desperate. You must make a large slit in the fabric. Both Peter and Sarah look frightened, and they are relying on you to make the right decision.

*If you use Sarah's plan
and pull together on the cord,
turn to page 4.*

*Perhaps Peter is right. A slit in the
balloon's fabric will let the gas out quickly.
If this is your decision,
turn to page 5.*

Lightning flashes and the four of you are treated to a frightening and spectacular display of nature's fury. As the night passes, the storm breaks and the moon appears from behind clouds. The night wind is warm, and far below, you see the silvered waters of the Mediterranean. Dawn comes with streaks of red and gold, and to the south, you see a hazy line of yellow, the coast of North Africa and the Sahara desert beyond!

Should you try to land the balloon near the shore where fishermen could help you, or should you drift further south toward the desert? There will be cities of white with minarets, cool oases with date palms and Arabs in flowing white robes. You take a vote.

If you all decide to land near the shore, release the balloon's gas and descend to page 6.

But if the lure of the Sahara is too strong to stop your flight, put on some suntan lotion and drift south toward page 8.

You all pull together. Even Harry is able to tug on the end of the cord. You hear the slow hiss of escaping gas. But without warning, the cord breaks. Cold wind and rain are soaking you and lightning flashes. You attempt to slit the fabric with Peter's knife. The knife slips from your chilled fingers. The balloon is lower now, sweeping over a village. A church spire looms closer and closer. You brush past it, startling pigeons perching on the gutters of the roof. Beyond the village you see a sandy beach, anchored fishing boats and the sea beyond. You must do something!

Sarah suggests that you toss out the anchor with its long rope. Perhaps you can snag something.

The danger is that a quick stop might rip the basket apart!

If you decide to drop the anchor, turn to page 10.

If you decide to do nothing and hope that the local fishermen will come to your rescue when the balloon settles into the water, turn to page 9.

You take Peter's knife and climb up on his shoulders. The balloon is swinging wildly in the winds of the storm. Reaching as far as you can, you puncture the silk of the balloon. Gas starts to escape in a rush. You look down from Peter's shoulders just in time to see the waves reach up and grab the balloon's wicker basket. Harry howls in terror. As the wicker basket lands in a cloud of spray, you are thrown clear. You sink into the churning sea for what seems like minutes and then slowly rise to the surface. The balloon is nowhere in sight, hidden by the moving mountains of water. You strike out in what you hope is the right direction.

Take a large gulp of air and turn to page 14.

Looking up and down the shoreline, you realize that you have landed on a very remote section of the North African coast. Nothing except sand and low, scrubby hills can be seen in either direction. But it certainly feels good to be back on solid ground again. Eagerly, you all start to explore your

surroundings. Harry finds an interesting bush, but it is Peter who spies the entrance to a cave which overlooks the beach. Just as you start to climb toward the cave, a dozen horsemen in white robes thunder over the top of a sand dune and ride toward you, shouting and waving swords.

If you decide to accept capture, raise your hands in surrender, put on a good smile and hope for the best on page 12.

But if you think the horsemen are dangerous, hide in the cave that Peter has discovered on page 19. And watch your head as you crawl through the narrow entrance to the mysterious cave!

8

The endless, golden sands of the Sahara drift beneath you. After the cold night, the hot sun feels good. You see caravans with hundreds of camels, sheltered oases and mud-walled villages. Sarah gives a shout of surprise, for there to the south is a great mound of silver. As you drift closer, you see that it is a domed, metal machine with hundreds of portholes set along its rim.

Should you descend and land? This must be a flying saucer, and perhaps you will be the first to meet space travelers. But Peter cautions you to drift on. Travelers from outer space may be dangerous.

If you decide to land, pull the cord and descend to page 16.

But if you decide to play it safe, hope that the space travelers won't see you and drift on to page 17.

The storm has swallowed up the light and it is getting dark. The balloon is slowly descending toward the angry sea. You catch a last glimpse of the shoreline. It seems only a mile or so away. And then you crash down into the sea. There is a tumbling of bodies. The wicker basket of the balloon is partially filled with water but still floating. Peter and Sarah cling to each other with fright and cold. Should you swim for shore to direct the rescue effort by the fishermen, or should you stay with your friends? They look to you for a decision.

Perhaps you should swim for shore. You have always been a strong swimmer. If this is your decision, turn to page 14.

But maybe you should stay with your friends and await rescue. If this is what you decide, turn to page 22.

You and Peter heave the anchor over the side. The rope snakes out rapidly. Far below you, the anchor bounces off a cobblestone street and through a flower bed, and drags across the sandy beach. It is too late for the anchor to catch on anything! Just as you lose hope, the anchor, which is now dragging through the water, catches on a small boat. There is a violent shock as the balloon whips the end of the anchor line taut. For a second the balloon strains on the end of the rope like a dog on a leash. But seconds later you see the boat has broken loose and is being towed behind the balloon. At least you will have something to shelter in when the balloon finally settles into the raging sea. But should you slide down the rope to the deck of the boat now, or wait for morning?

If you decide to slide down the rope now, turn to page 20.

But if you decide to wait for the storm to abate and for morning to come, turn to page 18.

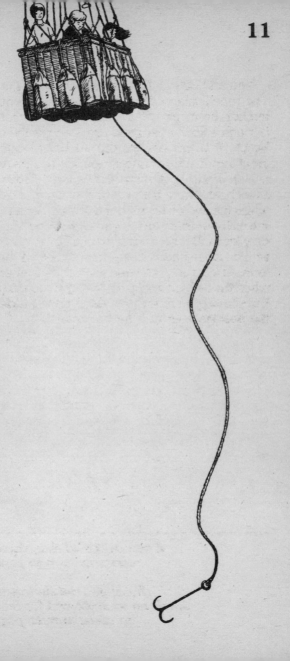

The dozen horsemen reign up next to you in a shower of sand. The men are dark and fierce-looking, with brilliant white teeth and deep-set eyes. In a strange language, they command you to get on a horse. With Harry trotting proudly beside you, the riders turn back into the desert. For hours, there is only the sound of leather creaking and the hollow echo of hooves on barren rock and sand. They follow a path through a narrow canyon, guarded by desert tribesmen who stand high above on rock ledges, holding rifles and watching the horizon. You have entered their desert stronghold!

The valley opens out and soon you see parched fields of wheat and large, open ponds of water. Finally, you enter a white city, surrounded by high mud walls.

You are taken to a large house. As you enter, you see that it is a palace with an open courtyard in the center, green plants growing everywhere and colorful birds singing from nearly every branch. Friendly servants come and bring you food and drink. But every door is guarded by one of the desert tribesmen.

Go on to the next page.

At last, a man enters, dressed in red robes with a silver-headed dagger on one side and a sword slung from the other.

"Greetings, honored guests," he says in a deep voice. "It is the fate of Allah that you have come to my kingdom. Perhaps it is also fate that you hold the key to my victory against hateful men who have invaded my desert kingdom.

"Will you join me in my fight against these evil people, or must I return you to the shore of the Mediterranean? The choice is yours, and I will do you no harm if you do not accept."

If you join the chieftain, turn to page 51.

But if you feel that this sounds too risky, tell the desert chieftain that you wish to return to the North African coast and turn to page 52.

At first your strokes are strong and sure. But you have never swum in mountainous seas like this. From the top of a wave, you catch sight of the shore, but then a wave, larger than the rest, breaks over you, filling your mouth and nose with sea water. You panic. You'll never make it, swimming against the seas and wind!

**This Could Be The End,
but it doesn't have to be
if you go on to page 15.**

But then you remember that if you lay on your back with your lungs full of air and arms and legs outstretched, you'll float like a cork. You try this and find it much easier. The sky whirls around as you are tossed from wave to wave. It seems like a very long time but finally, you hear your dog, Harry, barking excitedly. You lift your head and there, only a few waves away, is the balloon. With thanks in your heart, you swim the last few strokes and your friends pull you aboard. Harry, who saved you, licks your face. You rest, huddled together, waiting for the dawn.

After a cold and sleepless night,
turn to page 22.

Lower and lower you drift. Finally, you settle to earth and the spacemen surround you. You see that although their ears are nearly as large as their hands and flap excitedly, their faces are smiling. They all point to Harry and you realize that they think Harry is your leader, because of his big ears. One man with very large ears motions Harry to follow him. And all of you follow Harry, wishing that your ears were big and floppy.

The man leads you to a silver dome and, after bowing low to Harry who calmly wags his tail, directs you to enter. And as you stand there expectantly, a red mist hisses from hidden pipes, and you fall to the floor, asleep.

*Rest for awhile and then awake,
completely refreshed, to meet
the spacemen's leader on page 34.*

For a minute, you think you are safe. The balloon makes no sound and you are nearly past the flying saucer's landing place. But the shadow of the balloon drifts across the saucer and you see men looking up. A white light flares and before you can do anything, a hole burns in the balloon's fabric. Down you go to a hard landing. Soon, you are surrounded by men in blue spacesuits. They are smaller than you and very strong. Several of them shout, *"Gleeb Fogo, Gleeb Fogo!"* They shove you into a metal hut and the door slams behind you. Harry starts to burrow excitedly in the dirt floor, and you realize that he is trying to dig an escape tunnel. Perhaps it is better to wait to see what your captors want of you. Possibly, they come in peace.

If you decide to follow Harry down his tunnel, give him a hand and crawl to page 37.

But if you decide to wait to see what happens when your captors come to question you, be patient and go to page 38.

A long night passes. The storm slowly abates. The black clouds part to reveal a sky full of stars and a slipper moon. Trailing far behind and below you, is the small boat, its wake silver in the moonlight. Toward dawn, you and your friends fall asleep. You awake to shouting. As you peer over the rim of the basket, you see a man with a full black beard on the deck of the boat shaking his fist at you. He takes the line which is caught in his boat's rigging and wraps it around a winch. Slowly, he reels you in, as if you were a giant puffer fish. Harry growls deep in his throat, as though he senses danger.

Should you accept capture? After all, it is your fault that the man's boat has been torn loose from its anchor. Perhaps he will accept your apology and offer you food and drink. If this is your choice, turn to page 41.

Sarah is more cautious. She points out that the man is dangerous-looking and very angry. Wouldn't it be safer, she says, if we were to cut loose and let the balloon sail on? Land can't be far away, and all of you feel more confident, now that the storm is gone and the sun is rising. If this is your decision, turn to page 3.

As you all lie panting in the cave from your hard run, you hear the horsemen thunder by. "They didn't see us after all!" Peter exclaims. Cautiously, you peer out the opening. The horsemen continue on for a moment and then circle back. It looks like they did see you at first, and then lost sight of you as you scrambled for the cave.

"They'll start to search for us soon," Sarah says. "What will we do?"

You can see their bright swords in the sunlight. Their leader, dressed in purple robes, wheels his horse around and points directly at your cave. Other horsemen start to dismount and climb the hill toward you.

"Look," Peter shouts. "There are old doors here in the cave." You examine the doors. There are three of them and each is painted a different color. Perhaps they are storage vaults for smugglers, or even the entrance to tunnels. You had better choose one of them and hide.

If you open the Blue Door, enter it quickly and turn to page 24.

Peter thinks the Red Door is best. If you think his hunch is correct, enter the Red Door and lock it behind you on page 28.

Sarah and Harry pick the White Door. What a difficult decision, but if this is your choice, be quick about it and turn to page 27.

Peter and Sarah first slide down the rope. Harry climbs on your shoulders and you work your way down to the deck of the small sailing craft. Peter checks below deck and then reports (with a snappy salute) that there is no one aboard, and that there is plenty of food and water on board.

The first order you give is to cut away the balloon. It is pulling the boat too fast and spray is sizzling over the desk.

Sarah thinks that you should turn the boat around, raise the sails and beat back against the wind to the coast of France.

But Peter is keen to go on. To the south, he says, is the golden coast of Africa, with desert sheiks, caravans and all sorts of adventure.

Both look to you for a decision, but you smile and pull a coin from your pocket. "Let the coin decide," you laugh, and flip it in the air.

"Heads" and you shall try to return to the coast of France.

"Tails" and you will carry on to the south and the coast of Africa.

The coin lands on the deck.

If it is "Heads," turn to page 81.

If it is "Tails," turn to page 82.

Dawn comes slowly, turning the eastern sky pink. You are all miserable, and you share what little food remains, hoping that rescue will come soon. You each take turns clinging to the rim of the basket, looking for the fishermen. Sarah, who is on lookout, suddenly gives a cry of surprise and points to the south. There, you all see the menacing shape of a submarine running on the surface. Men move on deck, and a black flag flies from the conning tower. Could it be a pirate submarine?

You must decide whether to shout for help and hope that the submarine's crew are friendly, or whether you must crouch down and hope that they don't notice you. Surely fishermen will find you before nightfall.

If you decide to shout to the submarine's crew, turn to page 23.

If you decide to hide and wait for the fishermen, turn to page 26.

All three of you shout together and you wave your shirt. The sub continues onward and you think that they have not seen you. At last, a man points to you and the sub alters its course toward you. Minutes later you are standing, dripping wet and cold, on the deck. A man in a white wool sweater and dark jacket climbs down from the conning tower and approaches. He is deeply tanned and his face, although heavily scarred, has a look of intelligence.

"Good luck for all of you, I'll wager," he growls. "But we can't be spotted on the surface. We're submerging in ten minutes. If you swear to keep our secret, I'll let you stay. Otherwise, we can only give you some food, water and a small rubber raft. There's an island to the west and it's an easy row. Quickly now, what's your decision, my hearties?"

If you decide to swear secrecy and stay aboard the sub, turn to page 33.

If you decide that they are pirates, and you want to row to the shelter of the island, turn to page 32.

You and your friends push and tug at the Blue Door. Slowly, it creaks open to reveal a staircase leading downward. Although there are no light bulbs, the staircase and the dirt walls around you glow with a soft light. On tiptoes, all of you descend. At the bottom, there is a wooden landing and an underground river flowing rapidly by. A small rowboat is tied up to the landing. Perhaps you should use the boat to explore the underground river? Then Peter shouts that he has found a path which leads upstream, right beside the rushing waters. Which way shall it be?

Going downstream in the boat sounds easier than walking. If this is your choice, get into the boat with your friends and let the boat drift downstream to page 36.

But maybe going upstream would be exciting. The river has to come from somewhere. If this is your choice, tighten the laces on your shoes and start walking upstream to page 89.

The submarine passes from sight. All morning and through the afternoon, you take turns standing watch, looking for the fishermen or a passing ship. As evening falls, you see a freighter on the horizon and you shout for help, but the ship does not alter course toward you. Fog settles over the water and to stay alive through the night, you hug each other for warmth. The next day is foggy. You hear the sounds of small fishing boats searching for you, blowing their horns. But no one finds you. Another day passes. And another. Your food and water are gone.

The fifth day dawns, hot and clear. The sun beats down but no fishing boats come. You understand that you will end your journey here. Sharks swim in restless circles around the waterlogged wicker basket.

The End

You enter through the White Door and lock it behind you. It is very dark and in the far distance, you can hear strange music. Finally, your eyes adjust to the darkness and you can see pinpoints of stars! And planets with rings of color floating in the black, inky void of space.

As you walk along a pathway, you see strange, partially formed visions . . . of black rivers rushing through rocky tunnels, of jewels and chests of gold, of green, snow-capped mountains and stormy blue seas. A voice says in your mind that you have entered a time-shift . . . that you can move forward or backward in both time and space. Your friends hold tightly to your arm, wondering what to do. A comet burns across the sky and you feel the cold rain of meteor dust. It would be better to leave this strange place and frantically, your mind reaches out to grasp a vision.

Now warp through space and time to either a stormy night at sea on page 18, or an underground river on page 36.

The Red Door swings open on well-oiled hinges. You step into a clean, well-lighted corridor. The air is cool and air-conditioned, and the place smells like an office building!

The four of you tiptoe down the corridor and enter a large room. Along a wall, computers are whirring, and in the center of the room are several men and women in white coats, pouring chemicals into vats, looking through microscopes and making notes on large sheets of paper.

A small man with very thick glasses rushes up to you. "Goodness me," he exclaims. "This is a secret government laboratory. You shouldn't be here!"

You explain that it was just by accident and then ask, "What do you do here? It looks very scientific."

Go on to the next page.

The man, whose name is Professor Whachit, scratches his balding head. "I don't know," he says. "We've been working for so long that we have forgotten what we were doing. But we do have some inventions that we can try out on you." He shows you a jar of liquid. "I'm afraid that you can't leave here alive. It's so secret that we just couldn't allow that. But if you help us in our experiments, then we might trust you."

You and your friends look at each other. You really don't want to try drinking the Professor's secret liquid. Sarah whispers, "Let's run for it. Maybe we can find a way out."

Should you decide to drink the Professor's liquid, hold your nose and gulp down the foul-smelling stuff. Then relax until the chemical takes effect on page 66.

But if you think that you can escape from the Professor's laboratory, push Professor Whachit aside and run for the door on page 39.

Paddling backward sounds crazy, but Sarah is very confident. You turn the rubber dinghy to face the advancing seas. You find that you have much better control over the little boat. Nearer and nearer the reef you drift. The breaking seas sound like a continuous roll of thunder. "Now!" Sarah shouts. "Spin the boat around and row for the shore before the next wave breaks!" In a slick of green foam, you pass over the reef, jagged spears of coral just inches below the thin fabric of your dinghy's bottom. Looking back, you see a monster sea advancing, its top curling with foaming white water. It curls far above your heads, blotting out the sun. Now you are pulling on the oars as if you were being chased by a screaming demon. The sea breaks, and a wall of foaming water rushes at you. But you are safe inside the lagoon, and the foam's fury has been broken by the reef. You all sigh and rest on the oars, glad to be alive. Finally, with weary arms, you resume rowing toward the shore. Those waving palm trees still seem miles away.

Wipe the sweat from your face, keep rowing and turn to page 32.

"This way," Peter shouts. He takes one of the oars and you take the other. Sitting side by side, you use your oars as paddles, scooting down the backs of waves and then climbing up the crests. You are almost to the reef. Peter takes a quick look backward. "Now!" he shouts. "Paddle fast!" But you have gotten your oar in the wrong position, and instead of biting into the water it just splashes without effect. And suddenly, the raft is going in circles. Sarah screams, and you look up for a split second as the sun is blotted out by the curling crest of a giant wave. Too late! The wave breaks, dumping tons of foaming water. You whirl in a wet blackness, the water sucking air from your lungs. Your last thought is that you hope your friends will forgive you for your mistake in handling the paddle. Your journey is finished.

The End

It looks like a long row. Sometimes, the island is lost behind the heaving waves. Peter directs you, as he remembers that the island is just a little to the left of the rising sun. Soon, all of you can see palm trees and low hills. In a rumble of surf, your boat lands on the beach.

There must be a fishing village nearby, but you decide to shelter in caves which speckle the cliffs, at least until you are warmer. You make your way to a cave. It is good to be out of the wind and the coolness of the dawn air. Slowly your eyes adjust to the dim light of the cave. There are three ancient doors, their paint flaking off and hinges rusty. One is blue, one is red and one is white. Perhaps food or warm clothes are stockpiled in the rooms beyond. Or even treasure! You all decide to try your luck.

If you pick the Blue Door, turn to page 24.

If you choose to open the Red Door, turn to page 28.

If you decide to open the White Door, turn to page 27.

"Good," the sailor says. "We're glad to have you with us. Come this way and I'll have you meet Captain Zud." You climb down through a hatch and are guided along dimly lighted corridors. A metal panel slides back noiselessly and the sailor guides you into the Captain's cabin. Captain Zud looks up from his desk. He is very old, his face weatherbeaten but kind.

"Welcome aboard my ship," he says. "What ye see and hear must be kept secret. My crew and I are tracking the whaling ships of the world, trying to preserve the great whales from extinction. When we find a whaling ship attacking whales, we attack the whaling ship!" He thumps his fist down on his desk. "We try to save the crews, but it's more important that we save our friends of the deep from this wicked slaughter." He points to pictures of whaling ships. Many of them have "X"s crossed over the photograph.

"Will ye take an oath and help me save the whales, or must I keep ye prisoner until we can find a place to put ye ashore?"

Sinking ships sounds wrong, but saving the whales is important. If you and your friends join Captain Zud, turn to page 44.

You had better not get involved with Captain Zud. Think of those poor sailors on the whaling ships! If you want to be held prisoner until you can be released, turn to page 67.

It seems like hours later when you awake. You feel wonderful and completely rested. A gong bongs and a short man with ears that hang down to his knees enters. "I am the Maximum Leader," he says in a deep voice. "We are space-time travelers, but we have run out of fuel for our ship. It is a common material here on your planet, and we have dug for it by boring with our laser drills, but we find only water and sand. This is the material we need," he says and hands you white crystals. You smell it and then taste it carefully. It's ordinary salt!

"There is a tribe of fierce desert men who live to the north," he continues. "In their storehouses, they have great quantities of this fuel. Will you help us in obtaining some? If you do not choose to, we will allow you to leave in peace."

This sounds exciting and if you choose to volunteer, step forward to page 76.

But if you don't want to get involved in what seems to be the beginning of a war, tell the Maximum Leader that you wish to go in peace and turn to page 77.

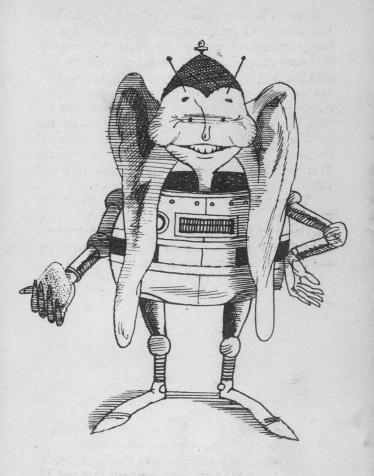

You drift down the river. The roof of the tunnel is covered with stalactites which glow in a rainbow of colors. Bats whir overhead, squealing eerily.

The river slows and spreads out into a large underground lagoon. The different-colored lights from the glowing walls of the grotto are amazing and all of you arch your necks, gawking at the fantastic display.

"Listen," Sarah whispers. You all listen and from far off, you hear a muffled roar. Somewhere up ahead, the river must tumble over a cliff. Near the far end of the underground lagoon, you find that the river branches left and right. Which one to take? A wrong decision might be dangerous.

It's too difficult a decision to make. You had better leave it up to fate and flip a coin.

If it's "Heads," steer your rowing boat into the right-hand passageway and hope for the best on page 61.

"Tails" it is. Well, let's hope that the coin was really lucky. That rumbling of falling water sounds awfully close. You guide the boat into the left-hand passage and float downstream to page 78.

Harry has almost disappeared down the tunnel he is digging. Sand and dirt fly from his hind paws. Peter, Sarah and you push the earth back into the hut and enlarge the hole so that you can follow. Suddenly from deep within the tunnel, Harry gives a howl of terror and then is silent. What has happened to your friend? Quickly, you follow and within seconds of entering the tunnel, you feel the floor of the tunnel give way. You fall to a soft dirt floor, followed by Peter and Sarah, who crash down on top of you.

Peter turns on his small, battery-powered light and you realize that you have fallen into an ancient mine tunnel. But which way to turn in your escape? The spacemen will soon discover your absence and follow you. Should you go left or right along the tunnel?

If you and your friends turn left, scramble along the tunnel to page 53.

But if you turn right, run to page 54.

At last, the door opens. A man lets you out into the evening dusk. *"Gleeb Fogo,"* he says, shaking your hands. He pokes you with his long fingers and is delighted when you squirm in laughter.

Following him, you enter a vast inflated dome, where hundreds of the spacemen and women sit eating in what appears to be a cafeteria. You all get into line.

He points to a pink mush which he calls *"Gleeb Mugga."* Next, he drinks from a cup of green liquid and says, *"Gleeb Orfit."* And near the end of the line, where there are many-colored plates of food which must be dessert, he says, *"Gleeb Fogo."* Then he leads you to a kitchen where the men who are cooking push you toward a large door. You suddenly realize that it is the door to an oven and you are *"Gleeb Fogo,"* a spaceman's dessert. What a terrible end, but you hope that at the very least, you will give them indigestion.

The End (BURP!)

Quickly you leave the laboratory. Guards are yelling and start to chase you. It looks as though all the doors to the building are blocked off. Up to the roof! You climb the stairs, two at a time, huffing and puffing. Finally, you open a door and find that you are standing in the sunlight. A helicopter is parked there. You all jump in and Sarah takes the controls. "Which way?" she says.

If you choose to fly west, start the engine and zoom in that direction to page 42.

Maybe going east would be better. The guards are already on the roof and they have their pistols aimed at you. If you tell Sarah to go east, buckle up your safety harness and turn to page 80.

Slowly, your balloon is reeled in. At last, the basket is just a few feet above the deck and you jump down. Peter and Sarah hand Harry down and then you assist them to the heaving deck. Without warning, the wild-looking man casts off your balloon's line. Your retreat is cut off!

"My name is Wright, Professor Hardly Wright, Expert on Ancient Africa. And who might you be?" his voice thunders. You explain your misadventures and his scowling face softens. "Well," he finally grins, "I guess I can't complain. I was bound for the African shore at any rate. And maybe you can be assistants in my search for treasure. If you join me, I'll give you a share of the wealth. But if you don't want to join me, I'll inflate a rubber raft and set you adrift near Black Isle, a small island that we'll soon be passing. What's your choice, my young friends?"

Professor Wright doesn't look like any professor you ever saw. He is dirty and rough-looking. But you like his grin, and a treasure hunt sounds tempting. If you decide to join him, turn to page 45.

Black Isle doesn't sound very inviting, but after all, it's land and safety. If you decline to join the Professor and instead row ashore, turn to page 43.

Up and away you fly. The government laboratory slowly disappears in the distance. Sarah sets a course to the west, following the afternoon sun. Soon, the desert rises into foothills and then into a low mountain range. "Mountains here?" you ask. Peter looks smug. "Of course," he answers. "The Atlas Mountains. My father told me all about them."

In the late afternoon, Sarah sets the helicopter down gently on a snowfield. Dazzling peaks tower above you.

You drink water from an icy stream and eat berries from a bush. But the sun is nearly down. Perhaps you should camp for the night in a lower valley and explore more in the morning. But Sarah can't start the engine.

Your friends look to you. Should you stay overnight in the cold helicopter or should you try to walk down?

If you choose to stay, get back in the helicopter and shiver through the night until the sun rises on page 68.

If you decide to try to walk down the mountain's side, tie a rope to each of your friends in case they slip, and descend to page 114.

Professor Wright shrugs his shoulders. "Well, you're missing the fortune of a lifetime, but that's up to you." He inflates a black rubber raft and all of you crowd into it. The Professor points to a small island. "Row for that and you'll be safe," he says, and casts you off. Without looking back, he sails on.

Each of you takes a turn at the oars. It is further than it seemed and the sea is rough. As the island grows closer, Peter shouts a warning. There is a reef all the way around the island, and huge waves are breaking on the reef. If the raft is flipped over, you will all be ground to death on the coral! Sarah says she has often sailed with her uncle and knows a lot about the sea. She claims that you must face the breaking seas and paddle in backward, staying in the troughs between the seas. But Peter has tried surfing many times and insists that you paddle strongly toward the shore and let the breaking seas lift you over the jagged coral.

Harry looks at you with trust, wags his tail and then covers his eyes with his paws, hoping for the best.

If you use Sarah's plan and paddle in backward, turn to page 30.

If you decide to follow Peter's plan and try to surf in, turn to page 31.

Peter and Sarah want to join. So do you and Harry, who is barking with excitement. You all take an oath to serve Captain Zud. For months, you track the black whaling ships. Finally, off the Antarctic ice cap, you watch the whaling ships begin their attack on a helpless pod of whales. There will be a slaughter. Captain Zud puts you before a television screen. You can see the whaling ship as it moves toward the crosshairs etched on the screen.

"When the cross hairs are on the bow of the ship," he says, "push this button. That fires a special torpedo which bores a hole and lets the water in. Them whaling fellers will be so busy saving themselves from sinking that the whales will get away."

If you decide to fire the torpedo and sink the ship, turn to page 46 or 47.

But remember, that's a real ship. It must be worth a great deal of money, and destroying it would be a crime. Perhaps you should refuse and suffer Captain Zud's anger. If this is your decision, turn to page 48.

"Good show!" he laughs. "I'm glad to have such fine assistants with me on this treasure hunt." He shows you a weathered map, brown with age. "This," he says, snatching it away so you can't see many details, "is a map that the great Venetian explorer, Marco Polo, made. It shows the route of a caravan which was lost in a sand storm over six hundred years ago. That caravan was supposed to be worth millions. And I know where they tried to shelter from the storm."

You sail on with Professor Wright for two more days, dreaming of treasure. But somehow, you don't trust him.

Toward the evening of the third day, you sight the shores of Africa. And after anchoring the boat in a safe cove, you start inland over the sand. Without warning, a group of desert men in striped robes comes charging over a sand dune, firing their ancient muskets in the air.

Quick: Should you run and hide, or should you trust Professor Wright, who thinks these are friendly tribesmen?

If you decide to run for the shelter of some nearby foothills, follow Harry to page 50.

But if you decide to wait and hope that the men are friendly, throw up your hands in surrender and turn to page 49.

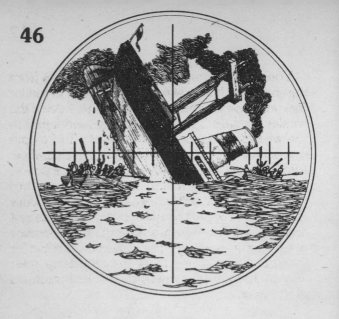

You fire! In a flash of foam, the torpedo streaks for the bow of the whaling ship. It strikes, drilling a hole in the steel. You can see confusion on the deck of the whaling ship as men run for the lifeboats. You have saved the whales!

And over the years, as the list of ships that you sink grows longer, fewer and fewer whaling ships put to sea. Now they are as extinct as the whales might have been. You and your friends live out your lives aboard Captain Zud's submarine, feared by all, but happy that the whales have been saved forever.

The End

You fire! The torpedo strikes home. Men from the ship launch their lifeboats in panic. You realize that you have committed a great crime. Even if the whales are saved, you may have caused injury to the whalers. You plead with Captain Zud to put you ashore, which he does with great reluctance. After giving yourself up to the international police, you are sentenced to jail. But during your imprisonment, you write a great book about your adventures. People from all over the world praise it and the governments of the world finally outlaw whaling. You are finally given a pardon and live for the rest of your life beside the sea with Harry, your dog, so that you can be close to the great creatures of the deep.

The End

You hesitate. The ship grows larger in the cross hairs. Captain Zud shouts at you to fire before it is too late. You turn and argue with him. "Wait," you say. "No cause can be so important that we risk the lives of men." And all the while, the whaling ship sails closer. Finally, it is too late. The submarine and the ship collide. The screen goes blank and, seconds later, water rushes into the compartment. You and your friends sink with the submarine.

The End

The men surround you, laughing. The Professor shakes their hands and then explains to you that it is the custom of these nomadic tribesmen to fire their rifles in greeting. What a relief! You whistle for Harry who comes back to you, looking very sheepish. All of you camp for the night and the next morning, you mount horses and head into the desert.

For days, you head south across the burning sands. Professor Wright does not stand up to the heat very well. He turns feverish and much of what he says is gibberish. Sadly, on the morning of the fourth day, he dies of brain fever. The tribesmen look to you for a decision.

If you think you should go on, find the map in Professor Wright's knapsack and take charge of the expedition. Perhaps fortune awaits you if you turn to page 57.

But this is a dangerous adventure, you reason. It may be better to return to the coast and try to find a way back to France, where you started your journey. If so, follow the tribesmen north and turn to page 56.

Harry leads the way with you, Sarah and Peter all close behind. The shouting and sound of muskets fades in the distance. "I don't think he was a professor, anyway," Peter says, catching his breath. "Yes," Sarah says. "I think he was just some kind of a cheap crook." You all agree but that doesn't tell you where you are or ease the hunger in your stomachs.

For hours, you climb through low foothills, and then as the afternoon shadows lengthen, you look down into a valley and see a small village. Would it be better to go to the village leader and tell him of your misadventures, or rather, should you all hide for the night in some deserted building?

If you think you should find the village chief, turn to page 95.

But if you want to keep your presence secret, sneak off and hide on page 58.

The chieftain smiles. "It is as Allah wishes." He sweeps his hand and the guards leave. "You are my guests. Follow me." You walk with him through crowded streets. Men smile at you and women giggle from behind their veils, but all are friendly . At last, the chieftain points to a pond. "You think that we water our crops from those ponds, but you are wrong. Those ponds contain salt water which we pump from wells. The sun evaporates the water, leaving us great quantities of salt. Then we trade the salt for goods which we need with the merchants who come by caravan. But now invaders have come to my kingdom and they are trying to take our only treasure . . . our salt. Will you take your balloon and act as our eyes, for you can see far distances from aloft, while my men can see only a few miles from the backs of their horses? However, if this is not your wish, you may depart in peace and may Allah be with you."

It is a difficult choice. The flight may be dangerous, but you are committed to help these brave people.

If you choose to help the chieftain, inflate your balloon and get ready to act as the Air Force of the desert tribesmen. Your mission is on page 70.

But if you wish only to continue on your journey, go to page 71.

You tell the chieftain that his fight is not your fight, and that you wish to return to the shore to find assistance from fishermen.

He slowly shakes his head. "I wish you had chosen otherwise, for I cannot allow you to carry away the secrets of our fortifications." He motions to a guard who approaches you with a strange smile on his face and his sword raised. You realize now that you have made a terrible mistake, and that you will never leave the desert alive.

The End

For hours you walk along the tunnel, guided by Peter's flashlight. At times, the smell of decay and damp are almost sickening. As you turn a corner, you come to a large mound of rocks. The tunnel has been sealed off by a rockfall. And Peter's light is now just a dim orange glow. Should you try to dig through, or should you return along the way you came and try the other direction? The three of you hold a quick conference. Sarah thinks that since you have come this far, you should try to break through. But Peter argues that you must go back and try the other direction. Soon his light will be dead, and stumbling through a dark tunnel is not his idea of adventure.

If you decide to try to break through, get your hands dirty and start digging on page 60.

But if you think Peter is right and you should retrace your steps, run back the way you've come to page 54.

Down the dark tunnel you run, slime making the floor beneath you slippery, and water drippings from the tunnel's roof spattering your head. Just as you think you have made your getaway, you hear shouting behind you. "GLEEB FOGO . . . GO . . . GO . . ." echoes down the tunnel, followed by a crashing sound. A ball of light and then another zings by your head. The spacemen are firing laser

bullets at you and your friends! With you in the lead, you crash into a wall. Dead end? Then your searching hands find that there is a fork . . . a branch to the right and one to the left. Pounding footsteps thunder down the tunnel. The spacemen are closing in. Should you go left or right? Your choice, and it must be a quick one.

If you choose the right-hand fork, get down on your knees to keep out of the laser bullets' path and crawl to page 101.

Choose the fork to the left, and run like blazes to page 106.

All that day you follow the tribesmen, who are strangely silent. Finally, the leader, Abdal, explains that his men feel that you have brought a curse with you, and that Professor Wright was just the first of many men to die.

That night you camp around a fire. In the morning, you discover that the men and horses are gone! They have left you to your fate. You have almost no water and no compass. Which way is north to the coast?

It seems to you that if you keep the sun on your back, you will be walking north. Harry, whom you know is a very wise dog, seems to want to go this way. But Peter claims that he is an expert in navigation. He says that if you keep the sun on your right until noon, and then keep the sun on your left in the afternoon, you will be heading north.

If you trust your own judgment, turn to page 86.

Peter always brags a little, but maybe this time he is right. If you think he is, and can swallow your pride, turn to page 88.

For two more days, you and the tribesmen trek over the vast wasteland. Using Professor Wright's compass and the ancient map, you come to a rocky range of low mountains. Following a canyon, you arrive at a dead end with tall cliffs towering above you. The map reads, "Dig by the silver-colored rock." And, indeed, there is a large rock with flecks of silver reflecting brightly in the sunlight. Abdal cautions you to be very careful. The face of the cliff is very steep and any digging might cause a landslide. But this is what you've come for, isn't it? If you work carefully, there should be no danger.

Abdal warns his men to back away.
It looks too dangerous. But this must be the place.
Treasure is just a few shovelfuls away.
If you decide to dig, cover your head with a
protective hat and turn to page 94.

So close and yet so far! Perhaps you
should call an end to the adventure
and turn back. If this is your choice,
retreat to page 96.

After night falls, the four of you tiptoe to the outer edge of the village and enter a building that Peter has spotted in the afternoon. Carefully, you push the door open. An oil lamp illuminates the interior. Stacked on the floor are piles of swords, bows, arrows and spears. You have walked into the village arms warehouse! Before you can retreat, a huge man fills the doorway behind you. He is wearing clothing of sheepskin and he wears a patch over one eye. In his hands he holds a sword and as you watch, he raises it. "Are you from *Gor* or from *Mir?*" he shouts. "Answer me now!"

You must think fast. One of the words must mean that you are friends; the other word that you are enemies.

Swallow hard and if you answer Gor, turn to page 64.

"Tell him Mir," Sarah pleads. If you follow her advice, cross your fingers and turn to page 65.

All four of you set to digging, Peter's small light held in your mouth. Loose earth and stones shower down on you. But unexpectedly, a blast of cool air strikes you in the face. You have broken through! Quickly, you clear away the few remaining rocks and scramble through. The four of you press on, climbing up the tunnel's slope toward the surface. As you round a bend, you see a pinpoint of light framing the tunnel's entrance. Minutes later, you look out onto the burning waves of sand of the Sahara. Peter thinks that it cannot be far to the coast and help. But just as you are about to leave the tunnel, Sarah cries in amazement. She has found another branch to the tunnel and this has small railroad tracks, as if the tunnel were really a mine. The set of tracks leads downward, but this branch of the tunnel is better built and well-shored up with wooden pilings. Should you try to lead your friends north to the coast, or should you explore the other tunnel?

If you choose to cross the desert, wrap your heads with kerchiefs to protect them from the sun and trudge north on page 88.

But if Sarah's tunnel excites your curiosity, turn to page 62. Just don't forget that curiosity killed the cat. What about you and your friends?

The roaring becomes louder and louder. You clutch each other in horror. Suddenly, the whole tunnel lights up in a flash, and to your right you see a steel cage with a gorilla roaring and shaking the bars! Another flash of light, and on your left a tiger growls at you from behind a bamboo fence. Darkness again. Cold, squirming things hang down from the top of the tunnel, brushing your heads. Ugh! Snakes! you think.

As you turn a bend in the tunnel, you find yourself in a lighted room. A very fat man rushes to the edge of the river and pulls you in with a long boat hook. He asks you for your ticket and then is very angry when you don't have any. He explains that this is an underground tunnel of thrills which is part of an amusement park owned by a wealthy Arabian oil sheik. You are escorted out of the park by the police and sent back to France. Too bad, because you and your friends thought it was more fun than Disneyworld!

Perhaps you should rent a balloon and start all over on page 1. If not, this is . . .

The End

Downward you go, following the tracks. The air is cool and has the faint smell of spice or perfume. Just as Peter's light gives out, you notice the gleam of brass on the tunnel's wall. It is an oil lamp. With fumbling fingers, you strike a match and light the wick. Now you have light!

Harry runs excitedly ahead and soon returns with something in his mouth. You examine it and find that it is a massive diamond, nearly the size of a baseball. Onward you rush, eager to find what must be the treasure of an ancient king. At last you come to a door. Should you open it? Perhaps danger lies on the other side of the strong oak planks. But surely, treasure is within your grasp.

If you choose to open the door, turn to page 63, but remember what happened to the cat that was curious!

*"But we already have a diamond,"
Sarah exclaims. "This is valuable enough to make us rich. Let's not go inside."
Maybe she's right. You can always find your way back to the surface. If this is your decision, turn around and follow the tracks back to the tunnel's entrance on page 104.*

The door creaks open to your touch. The smell of spice and perfume is stronger. You find yourself within a boxlike chamber, the floor beautifully tiled in jade-green glass. Diamonds, emeralds and rubies lie about the floor in great profusion, like toys at Christmas, scattered by some careless child. And as you walk further into the chamber, the door slams behind you. It won't budge. Without warning, a dim purple light starts to glow in the far corner. The light grows stronger to reveal a gold casket. The casket door slowly opens to reveal a mummy, which slowly sits up. A deep, muffled voice, old with the age of centuries, echoes across the chamber. "Welcome to my tomb; the tomb of King Ramsey the Great. I was buried here ten centuries ago in this, my treasure mine. You, who have found my tomb, are welcome to share in its wealth. And after you tell me the news of the past one thousand years, I may let you go, although I admit that it's lonely here and I could use some company." The mummy yawns. "Now, to begin with, tell me whether that crazy Pharaoh ever built those silly pyramids."

You hope that you can remember your ancient-history lessons! Unless you have a good memory, it is probably . . .

The End

"Aha!" he exclaims. "It is as I thought." With the point of his sword, he forces you out into the dirt street where other villagers surround you. You are shoved and pushed down a narrow alleyway. In front of a stone building, they force you to enter through a low doorway. The door slams behind you and you hear a bolt locking the entranceway. The smell inside is horrible, and only a trickle of light filters down from an iron grill set high in the ceiling. Harry growls and the hairs raise on the back of your neck. From the far corner of the room you hear a movement. As you watch, you see red eyes glowing in the dark. They are moving toward you.

The End

"Mir!" Sarah says, before you can answer. The man smiles and lowers his sword. "Ah," he says. "It is as our wise men predicted. You knew that *Gor* is the God of Darkness and *Mir* is the God of Light. And where, honored guests, is your light?"

Peter smiles and with a great show of ceremony, produces his flashlight. "Clatoo!" he exclaims and turns the flashlight on, the beam aimed directly into the man's face.

He cries out and falls down on his knees. Other villagers come and they too worship you. You are installed with great honor in a house overlooking the village, but you notice that the surrounding gardens are permanently guarded. You cannot escape. And each day, a different wise man comes and you shine Peter's flashlight in his face. Your flashlight is magic to them, but you wonder what will happen when the batteries fail.

The End

Gulp. All of you take turns in drinking the liquid. At first you feel fine and then slightly dizzy. Peter gives a shout of surprise and points to Sarah. "She's disappearing!" Sure enough, all of you are becoming invisible. Professor Whachit claps his hands in glee.

"Oh, goodie," he exclaims. "We had forgotten what that experimental liquid was supposed to do."

All of you are delighted with being invisible. You easily walk past the guards and away from the evil laboratory. Two days later, you return to your homeland. You find that it is very easy to get into movie theaters and sporting events for free, because no one can see you. But that is not very satisfying. People keep bumping into you and stepping on your feet. Eventually, you become police detectives. Because you can't be seen, you can discover what is going on without being detected.

The End

Captain Zud tells you that it will be a long time before he can put you safely ashore. "In the meanwhile," he instructs his First Mate, "teach them to operate the electronic listening device that helps us to follow the whales."

Every day, you listen to the whales as they move south in great pods. And after months of listening, you begin to recognize a pattern in their squeaks and grunts. "It is a language, just like ours," you excitedly tell your friends.

With the help of Peter and Sarah, you construct a computer and use this to try to understand the speech of the whales. After months of study, you finally learn their language! With Captain Zud's enthusiastic approval, you build an underwater loudspeaker and begin talking back to the whales. Soon they are telling you secrets of the oceans and the history of the Seven Seas.

Proudly, the submarine enters port followed by a pod of fifty whales. You call a press conference and astound the world with your ability to communicate with whales. Man's knowledge of the oceans, and his new friendship with whales, forever stops the senseless slaughter of your friends of the deep. And although you are now known as a great scientist, you mostly enjoy cruising on the back of a whale through tropic oceans, singing together the great whale songs of the sea.

The End

Dawn finally comes and the sun rises over four freezing friends. You get out of the helicopter and run around to get your bodies warmed up. The sun feels good. It shines with a warm, golden light on the slopes of snow above you.

"I can try starting the helicopter again," Sarah says. And before you can stop her, she presses the starter and the noisy engine coughs into life. There is a loud rumbling far above you and you look, horrified, as an avalanche breaks loose and roars down toward you.

You never had time to tell her that a loud noise can trigger off a snowslide. You start to run down the mountain, but the wall of snow overtakes you, burying you under tons of cold, white death.

A Chilling End

Willing hands help you inflate your silk balloon. Men, women and children gather around the basket holding it from rising as you and your friends make final preparations. The chieftain steps up to hug you before you leave. "Take care, my friends. See what you can see. Drift on the afternoon wind toward the interior of the desert. There, you will see many men and machines. We must know if they are advancing on our stronghold."

"But how can we warn you?" Peter asks.

The chieftain smiles and hands you a large mirror. "With this," he replies. "Flash it so that the sun it catches will shine on my army of men. Two flashes and all is well; three flashes will mean that the enemy advances toward us. We will be waiting for them." And with that, he signals for the balloon to be released.

Soon, the desert stronghold is a tiny speck in the distance. You drift over low mountains and across trackless sand. And in the late afternoon, you see a strange sight . . . another balloon exactly like your own! It must be from the enemy camp. Should you drift closer and try to talk them into making peace? Or should you get close enough to attack them; perhaps to use your mirror to blind them?

If you chose to make peace, drift closer to page 108.

But Peter tells you excitedly that warriors of ancient Greece used their shields as mirrors, and burned attacking ships with the concentrated rays of sunlight. If you attack, turn your mirror to the sun and focus the rays on page 72.

With a great deal of ceremony, you inflate your balloon. Just before you lift off, children come forward, shyly bringing flowers and bundles of food. The chieftain gives the signal and your restraining ropes are released. For a long time, you wave to your friends on the ground.

For hours, you drift south. Your eyes ache with the brightness of the sun, and your face suffers from the burning, dry wind. Harry lies panting on the floor of the basket, probably thinking of a cool stream to swim in. All that you see for miles are the bleak dunes of sand, rolling southward across the Sahara like frozen waves of gold.

In the afternoon, the wind rises, blowing the desert sand into a storm. On and on you travel, grit choking your throat. Toward evening, the storm dies and you see a mud-walled village. Should you descend and find out where you are? Or should you drift on through the night to see what tomorrow will bring?

If you want to descend, pull the cord which releases gas and settle down on page 74.

Yawn! You could use a good night's rest. If you want to travel on, curl up on the wicker basket's floor and awake on page 75.

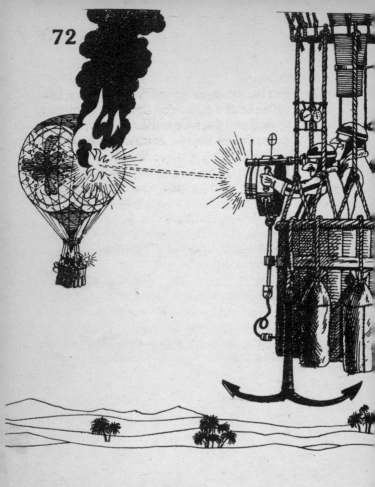

The sun is low in the west. Carefully, you use the mirror so that the sun's light falls on the other balloon. Almost immediately, the other balloon shines a great white light on you and your friends. You feel the scorching rays of heat, and in seconds your balloon is on fire and falling. Down, down you go. The desert floor rushes up to meet you.

The End

The other balloon fires at you! A gust of wind lifts you out of the laser's path. You aim your beam at the enemy and pull the trigger. BLATT! The other balloon collapses in flames, hurtling toward the desert floor, a glowing orange shape in the distance. You realize that you are free again to go on great adventures, but for your enemy it is . . .

The End

You yank on the cord and soon the balloon is descending. As the balloon touches down, you are surrounded by black natives waving spears and chanting in a strange language. Should you try to let more gas into the balloon and lift off? Those spears are sharp, and no one looks very friendly. But maybe it is just that you arrived in such a strange way. A friendly smile might help, and wouldn't you be upset if someone landed a weird machine in your own backyard?

If you choose to lift off, open the valve on the gas bottle and leave this desert village. Float on to page 84.

But Harry is wagging his tail. He usually knows when strangers are friends. If you follow the advice of his wagging tail, smile a lot and turn to page 85.

The night passes and a red-golden dawn spreads across the eastern horizon. And as the sun lights the land beneath, you find that you have drifted so far south that you are over the grasslands of Africa. Below, you can see herds of elephants and gazelles, running with the wind, and hippos snorting in the waters of a mighty river.

By noon, you are over foothills, facing a tall range of snow-capped mountains, in the south. Africa, you marvel! And Peter explains that there are many mountains in Africa. And great jungles, and thousands upon thousands of miles of grassy plains.

In the dying rays of sunlight, you set your balloon down gently in the foothills of the great mountains. There, men in white robes greet you and take you to a marble temple. A boy, sitting on a simple chair, greets you each by name. "I have been expecting you," he says. And he reveals to all of you the wonders of the universe. And you realize that this is not really the end but just . . .

The Beginning

76

"Zoot Gleeb," he exclaims with pleasure. "I knew that I could count on you. Inflate your space-traveling machine . . . a balloon, I think you call it . . . and travel north toward the desert men's stronghold. Some of my men will make a noise outside their walls and when the desert men ride out to investigate, you will use a laser pistol to cut a deep trench around their forces. They will be helpless." He rubs his hands together in glee.

"And then what?" Sarah says. "You won't hurt them?"

"Oh, no," he laughs. "We'll take their white crystals and leave ten thousand space credits in exchange. They might not be able to buy anything with the space credits right away, but who knows? . . . If they ever come to Gork, which is our planet, they can purchase all kinds of delightful things. Off with you now," he commands. "And take this laser pistol."

In less than an hour, you and your friends are drifting over the desert toward the enemy stronghold. Then Peter points to the north. There you see a balloon, almost exactly like your own. It must belong to the enemy! Should you allow it to drift closer and then possibly talk to them of peace? Or would it be better to just blast them with the laser.

If you choose to try peaceful negotiations, shuttle off to page 109.

But can you trust them? If you don't think so, attack by squeezing the trigger. Then see what happens on page 73.

The Maximum Leader sighs and then claps his hands loudly three times. Two spacemen enter the dome with laser guns.

"Blat these earthlings," he says in a bored voice. The men start to raise their lasers.

"But . . . but . . ." you cry, "you said that we could go in peace. You are going back on your word!"

The Maximum Leader yawns. "What a bore," he says, and sits down on a chair. "I have so much trouble with your language, getting the words right. What I meant to say is that if you did not wish to help us, you would leave here in pieces."

He flicks his hand. "Blat them, men," he says. "But please be careful not to make a big mess on the carpet."

The (BLAT) End

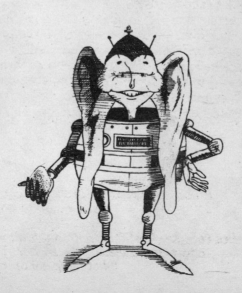

The rumbling becomes louder. Desperately, you and your friends try to cling to the side of the banks of the underground river, but the rocks are slippery and covered with moss. Faster and faster the river flows, and the rowboat whirls around and around in the roaring current. Just when the rumbling is so loud that you cannot even hear the screams of your friends, the rowboat shoots off into space. Over and over you tumble. You land

upright with a tremendous ker-splash. You are all soaking wet and scared, but thankfully still alive. The boat runs aground on a muddy bank and, knees shaking, you all get out. The mysteriously glowing rocks show steps cut out of the rocks leading upward. Should you follow them upward and abandon the rowboat, or take your chances on the underground river?

If you are afraid of the dangers of the river, climb the rocky steps to page 102.

But the roaring sound of the river is behind you. Perhaps it is safe to travel on by boat. If this is your decision, push out into the current and drift downstream to page 107.

Sarah can't get the engine going. And suddenly, without any warning, the guards fire at you. Long, sticky streams of red tape shoot from the muzzles of their pistols. You and your friends are completely wrapped up in the tape, until only your fingernails and eyebrows are showing. Captured! And what horrible punishment awaits you?

Professor Whachit sentences you to ten years of filling in government forms. You would have preferred breaking rocks or working in the salt mines. Eventually, you die of boredom.

The (YAWN) End

The coin jingles on the deck. "Heads" it is. All heaving together, you raise the sails. Sarah takes the helm and Peter works furiously with the navigational instruments through much of the next hour. Finally, he comes on deck and announces that in four more hours, you shall sight the coast of France. And indeed you do. Police and fishermen meet you at the dock, soon followed by television crews. What a story you have to tell! And as you stand there on the jetty, you notice that Harry is looking to the south, over the blue Mediterranean, tail slowly wagging. You imagine that you can smell the cooking fires of Africa and feel the searing heat of the desert. And, secretly, you wish that the coin had been "Tails." Perhaps if you could flip the coin again . . .

Return, if you wish, to page 21.

"Tails" it is and south you sail. "Steady as she goes," you shout with glee. Peter and Harry eagerly hoist the sails and Sarah takes the helm. With all well on deck, you go below to cook a whopping meal for your friends. It's a snug ship and a fine crew and, somehow, you feel at home on the bounding sea. Before strong winds, the little sailing ship flies, surfing down the backs of waves and cutting through their crests.

A day passes, and then another. And that night the wind grows stronger. The little boat is pressed to its limit, and you worry that the sails and rigging may not stand the strain. Perhaps you should pull down some of the sails. But before you can call to Peter and Sarah, there is a flash of breaking seas and a tremendous grinding sound. You have run aground! The four of you quickly inflate your life jackets. The small boat is breaking up in the pounding surf. A wave, larger than any you have

ever seen, sweeps you off the deck and into the foaming surf. Over and over you tumble, swallowing salt water. Is this how your adventure will end?

And then you feel sand beneath your feet. You wade through the surf and join your exhausted friends. Together, the four of you lie down in the shelter of a palm tree and sleep. At dawn, stiff and bruised,

you turn to page 6.

Quickly, you lift off. The natives, startled and then angry, throw spears at your basket. *Zit . . . Zit!* A few jab through the bottom of the basket, but no harm is done. You have escaped.

Soon, you are thousands of feet above the village, drifting on the wind to the south.

"We're high enough," Sarah says, and you try to turn off the valve which lets the gas into the balloon, but without warning it breaks off in your hand. Higher and higher you go. The balloon's fabric is bulging outward. It is too late to try to pull the release cord, or slit the fabric with Peter's knife.

Upward you soar, where the wind is cold and birds never fly. The moon, cold and unfriendly, looks down on you, and ice begins to form on the flowers. The petals break off as you touch them. And Harry howls at the stars. Soon, the air is so thin that you cannot breathe and you are cold, brr, cold.

The (BRR) End

The black natives soon back away, and a handsome young man approaches your balloon. "My name is Mum-abb-way. Have you brought television, candy or comic books?"

You and your friends look at each other. The natives want gifts and you have none. "Wait," Sarah says, and then hands the young man a bunch of flowers. "This is all we can give you."

The handsome man's face breaks into a broad smile. "It is good," he laughs. "We had those other things and threw them all away. Now our life is better, like the olden times."

All of you attend a feast that night and are given a hut to sleep in. In the morning, Mum-abb-way shows you the neat pens of cattle, the sparkling river on the edge of a forest where many fish are caught and dried, and fields of fruit and vegetables, all ripening in the sun.

After weeks of living with the natives, you are delighted with their simple life. They offer you membership in their tribe and all of you gratefully accept. Although the life is not exciting, you find that the peace and happiness of the community is more than enough to make all of you content for the rest of your lives. "Which," Mum-abb-way often says, "is enough for anyone to ask for on this earth."

The End

All through the day, you lead your friends, the sun burning fiercely on your back. Sarah shows you how to chew on small desert plants to obtain moisture for your swollen tongues. By late afternoon, just as it is growing cooler, you find a set of footprints in the sand. All you need to do now is follow them and find the desert tribesmen who

made them. But just before dark, you realize that the footprints have lead you in a circle. They are your own footprints! If you don't want to die, you had better follow Peter's suggestion. Through the bitter cold of night, you huddle together for warmth, and in the morning,

you follow Peter to page 88.

88

All day long the four of you stumble through the sand dunes. Calling a halt at noon, you take shelter through the hottest part of the day in the shade of a sand dune. At dusk, you rest again and all of you fall into an exhausted sleep. You awake with the stars glowing and the cold of night eating through your thin clothing.

"We must go north," Sarah says. "We won't be able to stand another day in the desert without water." But which way is north? Peter, confident of his success, says that the wind always blows from the north in the Sahara. You must face the wind and walk slowly. By dawn, he claims, you will all be safe on the shores of the Mediterranean.

Sarah says that he's wrong. She points to a bunch of stars which are formed like a dipper. "Use the two stars in the lip of the dipper and they point to the North Star. If we follow that star, we will be heading north."

If you trust Sarah's advice, look at the night sky and follow the star that she points out to page 93.

But if you think Peter's right, face the wind and start walking to page 92.

You carefully make your way upstream. The roof of the tunnel becomes lower, and sometimes you have to stoop to get through. The rocks and dirt on the sides of the tunnel are very loose, and you are often showered with small stones when your head brushes against the wall.

"I think we had better go back," Sarah says. "This tunnel is very dangerous."

"I think so too," Peter says. "There's so much dust in the air, I keep wanting to sneeze." And then without warning, he does. It's a tremendous sneeze. For a second, you listen to the sound echo down the tunnel. Then there is a rumbling. Peter's sneeze has triggered a rockslide. "Quick!" you shout. "Let's get out of here."

But which way? Loose stones and rocks are pelting down on you and the rumbling is getting louder.

If you decide to run further up the tunnel, move quickly to page 90.

Maybe you should go back the way you came. Turn and run back down the tunnel to page 112.

It sounds as if the whole world is coming to an end. Huge rocks are falling and the tunnel is collapsing. Suddenly, the roof of the tunnel gives way and a flood of water pours in from above. You are all going to drown. At the very last second, you all take a deep breath and start to swim upward into the black water. The pressure of the water is very great, and you feel like you are being crushed. Your lungs are bursting and you desperately need more air. But high above you, the water is lighter. Hold on, you keep telling yourself. The surface grows nearer and nearer. You might make it and then, suddenly, you are trapped in some kind of a giant net. We're finished, you think. And then the net lifts from the sea and swings onto the deck of a fishing boat, where startled fishermen separate you from dozens of tuna fish which they were netting. Your friends are exhausted but well. Harry shakes off the water from his coat and trots over to lick you in the face. That was a scary adventure, you think. And for all of us, it was almost . . .

The End

All night you walk with the wind blowing softly on your face. You grow more and more tired, stumbling along through the darkness of the desert. Toward dawn, the wind stops blowing, and then starts to blow from the opposite direction in strong, hot gusts. Soon, sand is being whipped up by the wind, stinging your eyes. Peter was wrong but it no longer matters. You have lost your contest with the cruel desert. You huddle together in a howling storm, as the sun rises in a fiery ball of flame.

The End

Through the night, the four of you trudge across the sand, following the North Star. And then at dawn, as you top the rise of a small hill, you see in the distance the refreshing waters of the Mediterranean Sea. Within an hour, you are all bathing in cool surf. Unexpectedly, a helicopter flies over you and then circles back as you frantically wave. Moments later, a handsome Arab officer helps you into the cabin, and you are flown directly to the government palace. TV crews record your arrival, and in days the whole world knows of your adventures. A film is made of your journey and all of you become famous and wealthy. But on hot summer evenings, when the wind is dry and the sun hangs like a ripe orange on the horizon, you remember the vast space and mystery of the Sahara, and secretly wish to return.

The End

Cautioning your friends to stand well back, you carefully start to dig. Because the earth is so dry, you make rapid progress. Just as your spade breaks through into a chamber, there is a deafening roar. The cliff is avalanching down on you. You will be buried in a tremendous rockslide unless you get out of the way. But which way? You can seek shelter in the cavern you have just broken into, but you may be sealed in forever. Still, you may have enough time to run back from the face of the cliff to the place where your friends stand in safety.

The first stones are pelting down on you. If you decide to take shelter in the treasure cavern, leap to page 97.

Your friends are screaming at you to run for safety. If you decide to return to them, run to page 96.

After watching the vacant streets for a sign of life, you finally enter the village. Smoke curls from many of the cottages' chimneys, but no one is to be seen, not even a dog or cat.

You knock at the door of a small, neat cottage. The door opens inward. The room is warm and inviting. Fresh flowers are set on the table and a fire burns in the hearth. But no one is there. On the stove, you find a pot of rich, thick soup. Harry nuzzles your leg, begging for food. You all know that when the owners return, they may be very angry, but your hunger is overpowering. All of you eat and then fall asleep on the rug before the fire.

Now turn to page 98 to see what morning brings.

You hastily join the safety of your friends. Without warning, a landslide starts and then is followed by a tremendous rumbling. The whole cliff falls outward, almost burying your little group. And as you look up to where the cliff had been, you see the remains of a beautiful city which had been covered by the sand and earth of centuries. Abdal bows down, as do his friends. He tells you in hushed words that this is the fabled City of Zimkaka. The buildings are splendid white marble. And statues of black men, fifty feet tall, look proudly to the sun. You have discovered one of the sources of the great black civilizations of Africa.

You return to the coast with the tribesmen leading. Soon, the whole world knows of your discovery. Scientists question you, and many nations in Africa invite you to honor them with a visit. In the end, you realize that the treasure you found was not just for you but for all men.

The End

Just as a mass of rocks bury the entrance, you scramble into the chamber. The opening is sealed, perhaps forever. You strike a match to see what the cavern contains. Nearby, you find a faggot of wood which catches fire readily. At least there will be some light. Near the entrance to the cavern, you find a vast heap of bones. And neatly stacked against the far wall of the chamber, you find hundreds of boxes and bales. Opening a few, you find only dusty leaves and shreds of cloth. Only then do you realize that the great treasures that the caravans carried out of Asia in Marco Polo's time were spices and silk. These have rotted away to nothing. So your adventure was all in vain.

The air is growing stale and the flame of the faggot is smoldering from lack of air. Your bones will join those of the caravan!

The End

You awake at first light. The fire has more wood banked over the embers and the smell of eggs and coffee awakens your appetite. You eat again, aware that someone must be caring for you. But no one appears. Then Peter shouts with amazement. On the mantelpiece is a large stack of gold coins. They weren't there last night and must be a gift from your invisible hosts. As you are trying to decide whether to take them, Sarah comes rushing into the house and says, "There is a schoolhouse in the center of the village, and it has a stairway which leads down to a tunnel. I can hear a loud humming."

Should you take the gift of gold coins and flee this strange and mysterious village? If so, turn to page 99.

But perhaps you should investigate the tunnel. If this is your decision, let Harry lead the way to the tunnel on page 100.

You put the heavy coins in Peter's knapsack and leave the village. For another day, you travel toward the coast and finally, in the late afternoon, stumble into a fishing village. The police there notify your friends in France and arrange passage by the weekly steamer which calls at the little port. But every time you try to tell of the strange village, you find that no words will come. The coins which you had placed in the knapsack have turned to small gray pebbles.

The End

Down the schoolhouse stairs you tread, each footstep echoing down the long tunnel. Harry is leading the way and you watch him in the dim light as he wags his tail and trots eagerly on. Soon, you come to a large cavern which is lit in a purple light. In the center is a space vehicle, silver-bright with dimly glowing portholes. A doorway in the space vehicle opens, and you feel no hesitation. You boldly enter. Within, the space vehicle's walls glow. An odd, mechanical voice says, "I am Ord Three of the Planet Anson. Those of you who stand here have chosen honesty instead of wealth. It is you to whom we give our trust. I and my fellow travelers have died in your year of 1781. But we were able to save three of our children who rest in suspended life, awaiting your care. Push the button in the center of the table and they will be revitalized. Let them live with you, and when you are older they shall repay your kindness with a journey into space and a visit to the Planet Anson."

Two days later, you and your new friends reach the coast of Africa. You explain that you found your three new companions wandering in the desert, suffering from loss of memory. But nothing can explain why their eyes are yellow and how they know a name for every star.

The End

On and on you crawl in the darkness. Peter is just ahead of you and Sarah keeps nudging you from behind to go faster, but the sounds of the pursuing spacemen are fading. They have chosen the other fork. And just when you think that you are safe, the ground rumbles beneath you and the dirt crumbles away to leave you falling in space.

Ker-splash! You hit water and sink far beneath before coming up. As you break surface, blue lights flash on. You tread water and gaze around you. You and your friends are in a deep well with perfectly smooth sides of glass. Rope ladders drop down from the top of the well and, thankfully, you climb up. The spacemen have captured you after all!

Pushing you ahead of them, they guide you to a large dome. And although they leave you alone, you know that if you try to escape again, they will deal with you very harshly. Sleep for awhile,

and then turn to page 34 to meet the spacemen's leader.

Carefully, the four of you climb the rocky steps. At the top, you find that the tunnel is level and paved with flat rocks. Onward you move, the cool green light from the walls of the tunnel illuminating your path. Suddenly, from behind you, you hear a rusty creaking and then a crash. You turn to find that an iron grill has dropped down from its hidden recess in the roof of the tunnel, blocking your escape back to the river. And as you test the grill to see whether it will open, you hear the identical sound from further down the tunnel.

Go on to the next page.

"It's the same kind of grill," Peter shouts. "We are trapped!" Frantically, all of you search for some hidden device to lift the bars, but you have no luck. Imprisoned deep below the earth's surface, you know that this is probably . . .

The End

But then you notice that Harry is squeezing under the bars. He makes it, turns around wagging his tail, and then goes galloping up the tunnel in search of help. Wait patiently for your friend to find assistance, and turn to page 111 to see whether you starve before he returns with help.

Upward the four of you climb, retracing your route to the mine's entrance. All of you are very tired, and at last you see the tunnel's opening. Stepping out into the desert light, you are nearly blinded by the sun. Without warning, strong hands pin your arms to your side and ropes bind you. Your eyes adjust to the brightness and you find that you are surrounded by soldiers in blue uniforms and white kepi hats. It is the Famed Foreign Legionnaires. But are you saved or are you now prisoners? A soldier with captain's bars and a patch over one eye steps in front of you, arms crossed and face set in a scowl. "Are you on the side of Prince Fudderdull, or are you against him?" he shouts.

You and your friends look at each other in confusion. Who is Prince Fudderdull? The officer draws a wicked-looking revolver from his holster. It seems obvious that you had better give him an answer—and soon!

If you think you're for Prince Fudderdull, gulp hard and then say so. You'll find out whether you made the right choice on page 113.

Prince Fudderdull sounds like a bad joke. And you and your friends say so. Now turn to page 115 to find out the wisdom of your choice.

Faster and faster you run. You stumble over stones and clods of dirt, which make a loose rumbling beneath you, and you realize that you are running down a steep incline. The tunnel becomes steeper and steeper. Peter screams and you hear Sarah cry in pain. Now you can't slow down. You tumble out into infinite space and, as you fall, you see the stars wheel in circles and feel the cool rush of time across your mind.

The End

On and on you drift, the river carrying you deeper into the depths of the earth. The glowing rocks cast an eerie green light, and you observe that the river is moving slowly and growing broader. At last, it seems that your boat is barely moving, but the river has become a vast underground lake.

"This must be it," Peter says. You ask him what he means. He tells you that many scientists believe there are great underground rivers of fresh water beneath the Sahara. "Just think," he says, "if the people of the desert had this water, they could grow enough food for all of Africa."

Slowly and carefully, you row along the edge of the lake, looking for some way upward. Sarah spots a passageway. Weak with hunger, you climb upward. Strange pictures of men and animals decorate the walls. Sarah says that these are hieroglyphics, the writings of ancient Egypt. It must be, she explains, that this source of water was known to the ancient peoples of the desert, and somehow the knowledge was lost in some sort of great disaster.

With barely any energy left, you come to the end of the passageway. Shrubs block the entrance and you bend them aside and look out. Nearby is a small, dusty village of desert tribesmen. What news you have to tell the world!

The End

As you drift more closely together, you are able to see that the other balloon is the same color and shape. You toss a line and the two balloons, like giant puffer fish in a crystal sea, drift together. The other balloon's passengers are just like you and your friends—exactly! Even an identical Harry.

Somehow, you have met yourselves through a time warp. The Other You explains that the "enemy" in the desert is a stranded band of space travelers. The fuel for their spaceship is ordinary salt that you buy in the store, but very rare on the planet from which they come. However, by blasting deep into the desert with lasers in their quest for salt, they have found great pools of fresh water.

The answer is obvious—trade salt for water! The desert men will be able to grow bountiful harvests, and the space travelers will have fuel. It is all arranged, and each balloon returns to its camp to tell the good news of peace and trade. The chieftain rewards you with honorary citizenship in the desert kingdom, and the U.N. honors you with a great prize. Kings, presidents and generals come to you for advice. And though you are happy, you sometimes wonder about The Other You. But when you look to the night sky, your eyes fall upon a certain star and you know.

The End

The other balloon draws nearer and nearer. You are amazed to see that the balloon is exactly like your own. As you get very close, it is almost like looking in a mirror. You are staring at another You and another Peter and Sarah. Somehow, you have warped through time and come back and met yourselves.

You have an interesting conversation with The Other You. It seems that the desert men need water—something the spacemen have discovered accidentally by blasting holes in the desert. And the spacemen need salt, something the desert men make in great quantities by evaporating sea water. So you arrange a trade—water for salt.

You return to the spacemen and tell them. They seem a bit disappointed that there won't be a war but, after all, a bargain's a bargain.

As a reward, the Maximum Leader invites you for a quick tour of the Solar System. You find it very interesting, but your seats are in economy class and the food is terrible. Everything they serve has too much salt in it.

The End

It seems as if years pass. You dream of fresh, cool salads, roast beef, ice cream and hot bread.

On the third day, you hear the sounds of running footsteps. Soon flashlights appear, led by a very thin and dirty Harry. Men, using saws, remove a few of the bars so that you can slip through. They are oil-well workers. Harry has run over 100 miles through the desert to their camp and then guided them back. "He just kept barking like crazy and then running off in this direction," one of the men grins. "We finally got the idea that his master was in trouble."

The men drive you back to the drilling site, and a day later a helicopter evacuates you to a city near the coast. All of you have fascinating stories to tell, but it is Harry who gets his picture on the cover of a national magazine. Soon he is a motion-picture star, but he doesn't forget his old friends. You are allowed to stay at his house and sleep on a nice rug. But you discover that you really don't like to chew on bones.

The End

The rumbling becomes louder. Great rocks are falling from the tunnel's roof. You realize that this is . . .

The End

"Good!" he says, smiling. "It is as I thought. You are friends of the Prince." He puts his revolver away, and over a cool glass of tea explains that he and his men are on a desert patrol to scout for the enemies of the Prince. The life sounds exciting. The patrol ranges far across the desert and experiences many hardships and also many good times together. You and your friends decide to join your newfound friend, Captain Best, in his patrol of the desert. He makes all four of you privates in the Famed Foreign Legion. And each morning for a year, you awake to the sound of a bugle and join the column of men, ready to march across the desert to a new destination and possible adventure. "Prepare to go," shouts the Captain each morning, as the desert sun rises. And off you march, sometimes going south and sometimes going west, always into the searing desert. When your enlistment is ended, Captain Best awards you and your friends with medals and you return to your home, full of adventure stories. At last, you write a novel about Foreign Legionnaires fighting in the African desert and call it *Go Best* in honor of your friend, the Captain. You make a fortune, but resolve never to travel the desert again without your sunglasses and a large supply of ice cream.

The End

The four of you carefully move down the mountainside. The cold night wind whistles through your thin clothing. And you always thought that North Africa was hot!

By midnight, you have reached the valley floor. A stream flows along the valley. Peter thinks that there will be a village upstream, but Sarah says that you should follow the stream because it always leads to the sea, and there will be large cities near the coast. They argue a lot about this, and finally look to you to make a decision. Harry really doesn't care. He is ready for any adventure.

If you decide to go upstream, walk to page 117.

Sarah is usually right. Maybe you should follow the stream down toward the coast. If this is your decision, whistle for Harry, who is presently chasing a squirrel, and plod downstream to page 116.

The Captain's face grows fierce. "Put them in chains!" he shouts. You are prisoners of the fierce fighting men, forced to drag a wagon loaded with supplies after the column of soldiers, as they plod their way across the desert. You and your friends get only the scraps of their meals, and are forced to sleep in the cold desert night without even blankets.

After months, the Legionnaires return to Prince Fudderdull's walled city. You spend the rest of your life there working as slaves. Many times, the Prince's enemies attack his kingdom. Neither side ever seems to win. And no one can remember the cause of the war. In the dull solitude of your cell each night, you scratch marks on the wall to represent the endless days of endless years.

The End

For two days, you follow the stream down the valley floor. The stream is joined by other streams to become a river. You camp at night under trees, and eat nuts and fruits which grow wild along the river. At last you see a modern city in the distance. Ragged and weary, you enter the city and tell the authorities about your many adventures. Television and newspapers make you famous overnight. One morning, as you are packing to take a plane back to your homeland, there is a knock at your hotel room door.

You open it and find a pleasant man with fuzzy white hair standing there. "I am a professor from the United Nations Ocean Exploring Committee," he says. He explains that the United Nations has built a submarine called the *Seeker* to explore the ocean depths. He and his committee feel that you have proved that you are adventurous and can handle dangerous situations intelligently. Would you care to join him on his journey under the sea? Of course you would! That sounds really exciting.

**The End of this Adventure but
the beginning of another . . .**

All through the long night, the four of you trudge upward along the valley floor, following the stream. Near dawn, you come to a small village. The people of the village have strange marks on their faces. Their skin is very dark but they have blue eyes and blond hair. Peter excitedly tells you that these are the famous Blue Mountain Men.

In sign language, the Blue Mountain Men tell you that they have no wish to be a part of the modern world. They will not allow you to go back to civilization for fear that you will tell a curious world about their existence. But they will allow you to join the tribe and live with them in peace. You are assigned the job of being goat-herder. A young boy of the tribe becomes your friend and teaches you to play the flute. Every day, you wander the hills around the village with your herd, playing sweet tunes and letting the sun warm your body. You and your friends are quite content never to leave this peaceful place and, somehow, you don't even miss the taste of ice cream.

The End

ABOUT THE AUTHOR AND ILLUSTRATOR

D. Terman was educated at Cornell University and Columbia University. He subsequently flew with jet interceptor and bomber squadrons, and went on to become launch crew commander for Atlas ICBMs. He has also served as a technical adviser to various government agencies involved in strategic and intelligence planning. In 1963, he bought a 77-foot schooner and sailed for the next twelve years in Caribbean and European waters. Terman now lives in Vermont where he divides his time between soaring, skiing and writing. He is the author of a novel of political intrigue, *The Three Megaton Gamble* as well as an upcoming novel about flying, *Points*. His next work, a sailing adventure, is in progress.

A graduate of Pratt Institute, *Paul Granger* is a prize-winning illustrator and painter.

CHOOSE YOUR OWN ADVENTURE ®

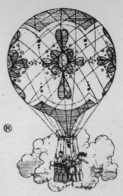

You'll want all the books in the exciting *Choose Your Own Adventure* ®️ series offering you hundreds of fantasy adventures without ever leaving your chair. Each book takes you through an adventure—under the sea, in a space colony, on a volcanic island—in which you become the main character. What happens next in the story depends on the choices *you* make and *only you* can decide how the story ends!

☐	23228	THE CAVE OF TIME #1 Edward Packard	$1.95
☐	23229	JOURNEY UNDER THE SEA #2 R. A. Montgomery	$1.95
☐	23183	BY BALLOON TO THE SAHARA #3 D. Terman	$1.95
☐	23180	SPACE AND BEYOND #4 R. A. Montgomery	$1.95
☐	23184	THE MYSTERY OF CHIMNEY ROCK #5 Edward Packard	$1.95
☐	23182	YOUR CODE NAME IS JONAH #6 Edward Packard	$1.95
☐	23185	THE THIRD PLANET FROM ALTAIR #7 Edward Packard	$1.95
☐	23230	DEADWOOD CITY #8 Edward Packard	$1.95
☐	23181	WHO KILLED HARLOWE THROMBEY? #9 Edward Packard	$1.95
☐	23231	THE LOST JEWELS OF NABOOTI #10 R. A. Montgomery	$1.95
☐	23186	MYSTERY OF THE MAYA #11 R. A. Montgomery	$1.95
☐	23175	INSIDE UFO 54-40 #12 Edward Packard	$1.95
☐	23332	THE ABOMINABLE SNOWMAN #13 R. A. Montgomery	$1.95
☐	23236	THE FORBIDDEN CASTLE #14 Edward Packard	$1.95
☐	22541	HOUSE OF DANGER #15 R. A. Montgomery	$1.95
☐	22768	SURVIVAL AT SEA #16 Edward Packard	$1.95
☐	23290	THE RACE FOREVER #17 Ray Montgomery	$1.95

DO YOU LOVE CHOOSE YOUR OWN ADVENTURE™?

Let your younger brothers and sisters in on the fun.

You know how great CHOOSE YOUR OWN ADVENTURE™ books are to read and re-read. But did you know that there are CHOOSE YOUR OWN ADVENTURE™ books for younger kids too? They're just as thrilling as the CHOOSE YOUR OWN ADVENTURE™ books you read and they're filled with the same kinds of decisions and different ways for the stories to end—but they're shorter with more illustrations and come in a larger, easier-to-read size.

So get your younger brothers and sisters or anyone else you know between the ages of 7 and 9 in on the fun by introducing them to the exciting world of CHOOSE YOUR OWN ADVENTURE™.

Bantam CHOOSE YOUR OWN ADVENTURE™ books for younger readers:

#1 THE CIRCUS by Edward Packard
#2 THE HAUNTED HOUSE by R.A. Montgomery
#3 SUNKEN TREASURE by Edward Packard
#4 YOUR VERY OWN ROBOT by R.A. Montgomery
#5 GORGA, THE SPACE MONSTER by Edward Packard
#6 THE GREEN SLIME by R.A. Montgomery

All CHOOSE YOUR OWN ADVENTURE™ books are available wherever Bantam paperbacks are sold.

AV3—9/83